Mark Haddon
Toni and the Tomato Soup

Gulliver Books • Harcourt Brace Jovanovich, Publishers

San Diego   New York   London

First published 1988 by the Penguin Group, London

Library of Congress Cataloging-in-Publication Data
Haddon, Mark.
Toni and the tomato soup/Mark Haddon.
p. cm.
''Gulliver books.''
Summary: Toni is delighted when a genie grants her wish for tomato
soup but soon finds that a little soup can go a long way.
ISBN 0-15-200610-9
[1. Soups — Fiction.   2. Wishes — Fiction.   3. Humorous stories.]
I. Title.
PZ7.H1165To   1989
[E] — dc19   88-16496

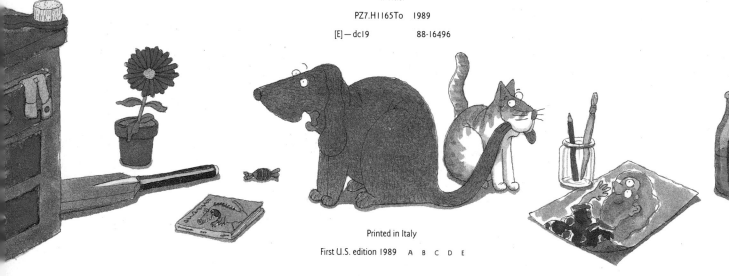

Printed in Italy
First U.S. edition 1989   A   B   C   D   E

To
Ali, Amanda (and Caspar), Andie, Ann,
Anna, Becky, Bert, Cheryl, Clive, Dad,
Dan, Dave, Doug, Fiona, George,
Grandma, Rev. Gilbert Márkus O.P.,
Helen, Liz (and Sebastian), Mary,
Mike, Mike, Mum, Nicky, Raich, Ric,
Sally and Theresa . . . and Julian.

Toni lived with her Great-Uncle George.

They got along very well.

Except at mealtimes.

The only thing
she really liked was
TOMATO SOUP.

Well, one evening,
after a terrible dinner
of meat and vegetables,
she was dozing
in her room.
Suddenly . . .

. . . a genie appeared!
"I'm the sneaker genie!
You have one wish.
What do you want most
in the whole world?"
"Um . . . tomato soup."
replied Toni.

Next morning, odd things started to happen.
Breakfast was tomato soup and a pot of tomato soup!

It was amazing!
When she turned on
the water to brush
her teeth . . . out
came TOMATO SOUP.
Mmmmmm!

The dog and the cat
found tomato soup
in their bowls.
So did the goldfish.

When Toni got to school, the class was learning all about tomato soup.

After lunch (tomato soup) the class went swimming.

On the way home
from school, it began
to rain . . . tomato soup.

She was soaked!
But there was no
water for a bath,
only. . . tomato soup.

Outside, it rained
and rained and rained
and rained and rained.

As the tomato soup flood began to pour into the bedroom, she lay on her bed and cried . . . big, red tomato soup tears.

"Toni! Toni!" shouted Great-Uncle George, "Wake up! You're late for school."

Toni woke with a start. I must have had a horrible nightmare, she thought.

"Coming, Uncle!"
she shouted, and
leapt out of bed.

Squish!